PARALLEL UNIVERSES

A SCI-FI LOVE STORY

ASHOK JAHAGIRDAR

Contents

CHAPTER ONE

The Fracture

The Fracture

Sonia had always felt that she was destined for something extraordinary. Her life in New York City cchfriends and family, she often felt an unexplained emptiness, like a song she couldn't quite hear. She worked as an architect, designing spaces that others would call home,

But her own world felt incomplete, as if she were missing something essential.

Neil lived across the country, in San Francisco, where he ran a small café tucked into a quiet neighbourhood. He was a quiet, introspective soul with a fascination for astronomy. Every night, he climbed up to his rooftop and stared at the stars, feeling an odd pull, a sense that he was somehow connected to something—or someone—out there. Neil couldn't shake the feeling that someone was waiting for him.

One summer night, a peculiar event unfolded in both of their lives. In New York, Sonia was working late at her office when the lights flickered, and she heard a strange, low hum. She looked out the window to see the entire cityscape momentarily bathed in a silvery glow, as though the universe itself had opened its eyes.

Across the continent in San Francisco, Neil felt an identical sensation as he gazed at the stars. The constellations seemed to blur and pulse, and for a fleeting second, he saw a face in the stars—a woman's face, vaguely familiar yet unrecognizable.

As quickly as it began, the strange moment passed. The city lights in New York returned to normal, and inSan Francisco, the stars settled back into their familiar patterns. Both Sonia and Neil rushed it off as a strange trick of the mind, a late-night illusion. But as the days passed, neither could shake the lingering feling that something had changed.

In the following weeks, Sonia began experiencing vivid dreams. In them, she was in a café, smelling fresh coffee and hearing the gentle buzz of conversation. She could see a man—always the same man—though his face was always just out of focus. She would try to approach him, but just before she reached him, she would wake up, her heart racing.

Neil, too, found himself visited by strange visions. He would be walking down an unfamiliar street in New York, feeling as if he were searching for someone. There was always a woman's laughter in the background, soft and warm, but before he would call out, but her voice seemed to vanish.

One evening, Sonia was out with friends when she spotted a painting in a gallery window. It was a street scene from San Francisco, with an odd, dreamlike quality that seemed to capture more than just buildings and sky. There was a café in the painting that felt hauntingly familiar, though she had never been to that part of the city. Drawn in, she entered the gallery and bought the painting, hanging it on her apartment wall.

Neil, meanwhile, found himself distracted in his café, unable to shake the feeling that someone was calling him from afar. His regulars noticed him gazing absently out the window, lost in thought. One day, while closing up, he caught his reflection in the window and saw, for just a second, a pair of hazel eyes staring back at him—a stranger's eyes, filled with the same longing he felt.

Sonia and Neil continued to feel this inexplicable pull, each sensing the other's presence, though they had never met. Their worlds continued, parallel but separate, bound by an invisible force neither could understand. Yet, deep down, they both knew something profound had happened, a fracture in the fabric of reality that had left them connected in ways beyond their comprehension.

Though they went on with their lives, each moment of quiet solitude was now accompanied by an inexplicable warmth, a whisper that they were not alone.

CHAPTER TWO

A Glimpse Through the Veil

A Glimpse Through the Veil

The city streets pulsed with life, but for Sonia and Neil, the noise around them felt muted. Weeks had passed since they both first felt the strange pull, that sense of being haunted by someone they couldn't name. Each night, as Sonia drifted to sleep in New York and Neil closed his café in San Francisco, the feeling only grew stronger. It was no longer just a vague sense of emptiness; it was an aching awareness, a certainty that someone was out there, close yet unreachable.

One rainy evening, Sonia took refuge in her favorite bookstore. She wandered the aisles, lost in thought, running her fingers along the spines of novels and poetry collections. Suddenly, she felt a surge of warmth, a strange comfort that was as unexpected as it was unexplainable. Her hand stopped on a book she'd never seen before, The Spaces Between Us. Something about the title gripped her, so she pulled it from the shelf and flipped it open. Inside, she found a passage about parallel lives, worlds running side by side, separated by only the thinnest of veils.

In San Francisco, Neil was cleaning up his café after closing hours when he spotted a book left behind on a table. The title was the same: The Spaces Between Us. He picked it up, intending to set it in the lost-and-found bin, but instead, he found himself flipping through the pages. When he landed on a passage that read, "Across every distance, a heartbeat echoes," he felt a chill. It was as if the words were calling out to him, reminding him of something he had long forgotten.

That night, they both returned home with their respective copies of the book. In the quiet of their rooms, they read the same passages, their thoughts unknowingly echoing each other's as if their minds were in sync. The more they read, the stronger the feeling grew—a magnetic pull, as if the universe itself were encouraging them to reach out to someone they had yet to meet.

It was only a few days later that the veil between their worlds finally lifted.

Sonia was walking home late one evening, taking a shortcut through Central Park. The sky was dark, and rain threatened on the horizon. She felt the familiar sense of being watched, or perhaps followed, though the path was empty. As she approached a small bridge near the lake, she stopped. Something about the place felt different, almost charged, as though the air itself were vibrating with anticipation.

At that exact moment, miles away in San Francisco, Neil was closing up his café. His routine always included one last glance at the night sky before he left, a habit born of his fascination with the stars. But tonight, as he gazed up, he noticed an unusual light flickering in the sky. He felt compelled to go for a walk, his feet guiding him down familiar streets until he, too, reached a bridge—the same bridge as Eva's, but in his own world.

As they both stood on their respective bridges, Sonia and Neil were seized by a sudden, overwhelming feeling. They each felt as though someone were standing just beyond the mist, a shadowy figure in the darkness. And then, as if by magic, the world around them shimmered, and they saw each other—not clearly, but as faint, ghostly figures in the fog. Sonia's breath caught in her throat as she saw a man's outline, his features indistinct but undeniably familiar. Neil stared in awe, his heart pounding as he glimpsed the shape of a woman, her eyes reflecting the same longing he felt.

They reached out instinctively, each lifting a hand toward the other. For a fleeting moment, their fingers seemed to touch, though they both knew it wasn't possible. The touch was soft, like the faint brush of air, but it was enough to send a jolt through them. In that moment, they felt a rush of memories—not memories of each other, but of feelings they had never been able to explain. Every glance, every dream of a stranger's face, every moment of inexplicable sadness suddenly made sense. They knew, without a doubt, that they had found each other across the impossible divide.

Before they could speak, before they could ask each other's names, the connection began to waver. The mist thickened, and their visions grew faint. But as the image faded, Sonia whispered, "I know you." The words reached Neil like a faint echo, filling his heart with a warmth he hadn't felt in years.

"I know you, too," he whispered, his voice barely a breath.

And then they were alone again, each standing on the same bridge in different worlds, the connection broken but the memory of it pulsing between them like a heartbeat. They each stumbled home in a daze, hearts racing, minds whirling with questions. Had they really seen each other? Was it a dream? A trick of the mind?

That night, they both returned home with their respective copies of the book. In the quiet of their rooms, they read the same passages, their thoughts unknowingly echoing each other's as if their minds were in sync. The more they read, the stronger the feeling grew—a magnetic pull, as if the universe itself were encouraging them to reach out to someone they had yet to meet.

It was only a few days later that the veil between their worlds finally lifted.

Sonia was walking home late one evening, taking a shortcut through Central Park. The sky was dark, and rain threatened on the horizon. She felt the familiar sense of being watched, or perhaps followed, though the path was empty. As she approached a small bridge near the lake, she stopped. Something about the place felt different, almost charged, as though the air itself were vibrating with anticipation.

At that exact moment, miles away in San Francisco, Neil was closing up his café. His routine always included one last glance at the night sky before he left, a habit born of his fascination with the stars. But tonight, as he gazed up, he noticed an unusual light flickering in the sky. He felt compelled to go for a walk, his feet guiding him down familiar streets until he, too, reached a bridge—the same bridge as Eva's, but in his own world.

As they both stood on their respective bridges, Sonia and Neil were seized by a sudden, overwhelming feeling. They each felt as though someone were standing just beyond the mist, a shadowy figure in the darkness. And then, as if by magic, the world around them shimmered, and they saw each other—not clearly, but as faint, ghostly figures in the fog. Sonia's breath caught in her throat as she saw a man's outline, his features indistinct but undeniably familiar. Neil stared in awe, his heart pounding as he glimpsed the shape of a woman, her eyes reflecting the same longing he felt.

They reached out instinctively, each lifting a hand toward the other. For a fleeting moment, their fingers seemed to touch, though they both knew it wasn't possible. The touch was soft, like the faint brush of air, but it was enough to send a jolt through them. In that moment, they felt a rush of memories—not memories of each other, but of feelings they had never been able to explain. Every glance, every dream of a stranger's face, every moment of inexplicable sadness suddenly made sense. They knew, without a doubt, that they had found each other across the impossible divide.

Before they could speak, before they could ask each other's names, the connection began to waver. The mist thickened, and their visions grew faint. But as the image faded, Sonia whispered, "I know you." The words reached Neil like a faint echo, filling his heart with a warmth he hadn't felt in years.

"I know you, too," he whispered, his voice barely a breath.

And then they were alone again, each standing on the same bridge in different worlds, the connection broken but the memory of it pulsing between them like a heartbeat. They each stumbled home in a daze, hearts racing, minds whirling with questions. Had they really seen each other? Was it a dream? A trick of the mind?

The Echo

The Echo

The days that followed were a blur for both Sonia and Neil. They went through the motions of their daily lives, but everything felt surreal, as though they were living in a dream. The world around them seemed brighter, colors sharper, sounds clearer. Even the smallest details—the taste of coffee, the smell of rain—were somehow imbued with meaning, as if the universe were reminding them of the moment they'd shared on the bridge.

Sonia tried to tell herself it had been a hallucination, a trick of her overtired mind. But no matter how she reasoned, she couldn't dismiss the feeling that lingered in her heart. She knew him, this stranger from another world. She could feel his presence like a gentle hum in the back of her mind, a constant reminder that he was out there, somehow connected to her.

One night, after another long day of questioning her sanity, she sat down with her sketchbook. Architecture had always been her outlet, her way of making sense of the world. But tonight, as she put pencil to paper, she didn't sketch buildings or blueprints. Instead, her hand moved almost of its own accord, and within moments, she found herself staring at a drawing of his face—the faint features she had glimpsed on the bridge, the contours of his cheekbones, the soft, intense look in his eyes.

In San Francisco, Neil experienced a similar compulsion. He had always been drawn to the stars, to the mysteries of the cosmos, but that night, he felt a strange urge to write. With a notebook and pen, he settled into the corner booth of his café, the same spot where he'd found *The Spaces Between Us*. Without thinking, he began to write about her. Her face, her laughter, the way her presence had felt like a balm to his soul, filling an ache he hadn't known was there. The words flowed effortlessly, as if he were transcribing a memory rather than creating something new.

Days turned into weeks, and Sonia and Neil fell into a rhythm, a silent conversation that neither could explain. They found that whenever they thought of each other with strong emotion—joy, sorrow, longing—the other would feel it, as if a spark had ignited across the distance. It was subtle at first, just a faint flicker of warmth or a gentle tug at the heart. But as time went on, the connection grew stronger, more vivid.

One morning, Sonia was sitting by the window of a coffee shop, watching the rain streak down the glass. She felt a wave of sadness, though she couldn't explain why. It was a deep, soulful ache, a heaviness that settled in her chest. She closed her eyes and, without knowing why, whispered, "Are you there?"

Across the country, Neil was closing up his café, feeling a similar melancholy wash over him. He had been thinking of her, wondering if she felt the same, when he suddenly heard a faint whisper in his mind: *Are you there?* He froze, heart pounding, as he realized the voice wasn't his own. It was hers. He knew it, deep down, with a certainty that defied reason.

"Yes," he murmured softly, as if she could somehow hear him. "I'm here."

Neil felt a rush of warmth in response, a gentle reassurance that filled her heart. She knew, in that moment, that they were truly connected. No matter how impossible it seemed, they had found a way to reach each other across the divide.

Over the following weeks, their silent conversations continued, growing more intense with each passing day. Sonia began to experiment, leaving messages for him in subtle ways, unsure if he would receive them. She would write his name in fogged-up mirrors or scrawl a note on a napkin, leaving it on her desk before she went to sleep. Each time, she would feel a faint echo in her heart, a feeling that he had somehow seen her messages, even if he couldn't respond.

Neil, too, found ways to reach out to her. He would play certain songs in his café, melodies he felt she might like, and each time he played them, he felt her presence nearby, like a warm shadow hovering just out of sight. He even found himself speaking aloud, his words soft and tentative, as though he were talking to her across the silence.

One day, he stood in front of the mirror in his small apartment and said, "sonia, if you're there, I just want you to know... you're not alone." It felt strange, speaking to an empty room, but he knew, somehow, that she would hear him.

Miles away, as Sonia stood in her own apartment, she felt a surge of warmth, like a gentle embrace wrapping around her. She knew, in that moment, that he was thinking of her. Tears filled her eyes, but they weren't tears of sadness—they were tears of relief, of joy, of knowing that she was truly connected to someone, even if they were separated by worlds.

The connection between them continued to grow, and they found comfort in each other's presence, in the knowledge that they weren't alone. Though they couldn't speak or see each other directly, their thoughts and feelings echoed through the dimensions, binding them in ways beyond explanation. They were no longer just strangers haunted by dreams and shadows; they were soulmates, bound across the fabric of reality.gh an echo. And for now, that was all they needed.

CHAPTER FOUR

Epilogue: Together Across the Divide

Epilogue: Together Across the Divide

Over the following days, Sonia and Neil each found peace in their strange, beautiful connection. They continued their silent conversations, sharing their days, their hopes, their dreams, knowing that somewhere across the divide, the other was listening. They learned to send each other echoes of happiness, of joy, of love, and those feelings sustained them.

Even though Sonia and Neil remained in their separate realities, they now understood the truth—they were not alone. They carried their love in their hearts. Though they lived in separate universes, they had found each other, truly and deeply, and that knowledge was a balm to their souls.

In each world, they celebrated the knowledge that somewhere, across a thin veil of existence, someone was waiting and caring. They knew they were loved, and they lived each day with the knowledge that, somewhere beyond sight, someone shared their joy and sorrow.

The ache of longing was still there, but it no longer felt like loneliness. It felt like love—boundless, enduring, existing across time and space. It was a celebration across worlds -it was more than enough.

The days that followed were a blur for both Eva and Ryan. They went through the motions of their daily lives, but everything felt surreal, as though they were living in a dream. The world around them seemed brighter, colors sharper, sounds clearer. Even the smallest details—the taste of coffee, the smell of rain—were somehow imbued with meaning, as if the universe were reminding them of the moment they'd shared on the bridge.

Eva tried to tell herself it had been a hallucination, a trick of her overtired mind. But no matter how she reasoned, she couldn't dismiss the feeling that lingered in her heart. She knew him, this stranger from another world. She could feel his presence like a gentle hum in the back of h that neither could explain. They found that whenever they thought of each other with strong emotion—joy, sorrow, longing—the other would feel it, as if a spark had ignited across the distance. It was subtle at first, just a faint flicker of warmth or a gentle tug at the heart. But as time went on, the connection grew stronger, more vivid.

One morning, Eva was sitting by the window of a coffee shop, watching the rain streak down the glass. She felt a wave of sadness, though she couldn't explain why. It was a deep, soulful ache, a heaviness that settled in her chest. She closed her eyes and, without knowing why, whispered, "Are you there?"

Across the country, Ryan was closing up his café, feeling a similar melancholy wash over him. He had been thinking of her, wondering if she felt the same, when he suddenly heard a faint whisper in his mind: Are you there? He froze, heart pounding, as he realized the voice wasn't his own. It was hers. He knew it, deep down, with a certainty that defied reason.

"Yes," he murmured softly, as if she could somehow hear him. "I'm here."

Eva felt a rush of warmth in response, a gentle reassurance that filled her heart. She knew, in that moment, that they were truly connected. No matter how impossible it seemed, they had found a way to reach each other across the divide.

Over the following weeks, their silent conversations continued, growing more intense with each passing day. Eva began to experiment, leaving messages for him in subtle ways, unsure if he would receive them. She would write his name in fogged-up mirrors or scrawl a note on a napkin, leaving it on her desk before she went to sleep. Each time, she would feel a faint echo in her heart, a feeling that he had somehow seen her messages, even if he couldn't respond.

Ryan, too, found ways to reach out to her. He would play certain songs in his café, melodies he felt she might like, and each time he played them, he felt her presence nearby, like a warm shadow hovering just out of sight. He even found himself speaking aloud, his words soft and tentative, as though he were talking to her across the silence.

One day, he stood in front of the mirror in his small apartment and said, "Eva, if you're there, I just want you to know... you're not alone." It felt strange, speaking to an empty room, but he knew, somehow, that she would hear him.

Miles away, as Sonia stood in her own apartment, she felt a surge of warmth, like a gentle embrace wrapping around her. She knew, in that moment, that he was thinking of her. Tears filled her eyes, but they weren't tears of sadness—they were tears of relief, of joy, of knowing that she was truly connected to someone, even if they were separated by worlds.

The connection between them continued to grow, and they found comfort in each other's presence, in the knowledge that they weren't alone. Though they couldn't speak or see each other directly, their thoughts and feelings echoed through the dimensions, binding them in ways beyond explanation. They were no longer just strangers haunted by dreams and shadows; they were soulmates, bound across the fabric of reality.

They learned to live with the ache of separation, knowing that, in some strange way, they were together. They each carried a part of the other, a piece of the other's soul, and that was enough to make their worlds feel complete.

They had found each other, even if only through an echo. And for now, that was all they needed.

दोस्तों ने भूत को पकड़ लिया

GHOSTS SERIES-1

अंश शर्मा

Made with ♥ on the Notion Press Platform
www.notionpress.com

पुस्तक लेखक

क्रम-सूची

प्रस्तावना

हेलो दोस्तों मेरा नाम अशं और मैंअभी 15 साल का हूऔर मैंदि ल्ली मैंरेता हूऔर दोस्तो यह मनै ैजो कहानी लि खी उसका आईडि या मझुे एक मवू ी सेमि ला हैजब मैंघर बठैा था अपनेफैमि ली साथ तो मैंएक हॉरर मवू ी देख रहा था तब मझुे आईडि या atha की क्यों ना ak हॉरर स्टाइरी लि खनेबठैे जाता और अगर एप्लोगी को स्टोरी अच्छा लगती हैजरूर सेसपोर्ट करना!

1

ओदोस्तो यह बात हैउस समय की जब मैकाफ़ी जायदा छोटा था तब मेरेपापा और चाचा भतू के बारेमेंबात कर रहेहोतेहैमेरेचाचा कहतेहैभतू सच मैहोतेमनैं उसेअपनेआखंो सेदेख हैलेकि न मेरेपापा कहतेहैअरेयार छोटे भतू नाम की कोई चीज़ नही होती यह सि र्फ हमारा एक वयम होता हैलेकि न यह सब बातेअपनेपापा और चाचा की नि खि ल सनु रहा होता हैऔर वो बाग कर अपनेदोस्तो के पास जाता हैऔर उन्हेंबताता हैकी तमुहेपता हैभतू सच मेंहोतेहैलेकीन नि खि ल के दोस्त भी नि कि ल के पापा की तरह बोलतेहैनही भतू नही होतेलेकि न नि खि ल को अभी भी लग रहा था की भतू होतेहैतभी नि खि ल अपनेदोस्तो के सामनेएक चलैंज रख देता हैनि खि ल कहता है की अच्छा तमुहेयकीन नही हैभतू होतेहैतो फि र हम कल साम पहाड़ के पास जो बगं लो हैंउसमेजायगें दोस्तो जि स बगं लेकी बात नि खि ल नेकी थी वो कोई मामलू ी बगं ला नही था बल्कि वो एक खाली बगं लो था जो की लगाबाग 100 साल सेखाली पड़ा था लेकि न नि खि ल को क्या पता और प्लान के मतुाबि क वो सारेदोस्त रात के बारा बजेउस बगं लो मैं जानेके लि ए इकट्ठेहोतेहै और जसैे ही बगं लेका दरवाजा खोलतेहैंगेट अपनेआप बदं हो जाता वोह सरेकाफ़ी जायदा डर जातेहैतभी नि खि ल का एक दोस्त नि ति न बोलता हैअरेहवा की वजह से दरवाज़ा बदं हो गया होगा फि र वो सरेधीरेधीरेअगं े बढ़तेजातेहैतभी नि खि ल के एक और दोस्त जि सका नाम रोहन होता हैउसकी नज़र कि चन मेपड़ती हैऔर वो कहता हैदोस्तो वो देखो कि चन मेंकि सी की फोटो टांगी है चलो पास चलकर

देखतेहैऔर वो सरेपास जातेहैऔर फोटो देखतेऔर उस फोटो मैखनू लगा होता हैऔर फि र नि ति न बोलता हैदेखो मनै तो पहलेही खा था मैंनही जाऊंगा बगं लेके अदं र लेकीन तमु लोग खा मानेऔर यह खनू पक्का भतू नेही कि या हैनि खि ल की वजह सेहमेंबगं लेके अदं र अन्ना पड़ा फि र नि खि ल और नि ति न को संतं करतेहुए राहुल बोलता हैदोस्तो अभी यह समय लड़नेजगड़नेखा नही हैबल्की येसोचनेखा हैकी क्या सच मै भतू नेही इस फोटो मैखनू लगाया हैऔर अगर भतू इस बगं लेमैंहैतो भतू वो कैसा दि खता होगा फि र नि ति न उस फोटो को उठता हैऔर उस फोटो मैलि खर आता हैतमु यह सेचलेजाओ दोस्तो सोचनेवाली बात तो यह है उस फोटो मैंसि फ पति की तस्वीर बनी होती हैफि र थोड़ी देर बाद राहुल बोलता हैचलो उबर साइट वालेकमरेमैं चलतेहैलेकि न जब वो अप्पर साइट वालेकमरेमैंपोछतेहैउन कमरों मैंलॉक लगा होता हैफि र वो लोग डि साइड करतेहैकी चलो इन कमरों की चाबी ठुड़तेहैवाहा पर 3 कमरे बनेहुए थेलेकि न उन्हें3 कमरेकी चाबी नही मि लती फि र वो लोग 2 ही कमरों को खोलतेहैजब वोह पहलेकमरेको खोलतेहैतब उस कमरेमैंएक बेड पढ़ा होता हैऔर कुछ समाहन जब नि खि ल नीचेबेड के नीचेजाकर देखता हैतो वाहा पर फि र सेएक फोटो मि लती है जि समेबच्चों की फोटो बनी होती हैऔर फ़ोटो देखनेके बाद जसैं ही फोटो को रखतेहैतज़े हवा चलानेलगती और आवाज आती तमु यह सेचलो जोहो और फि र डर की वजह वोह सरेउस बगं ्लो सेभर नि कल जातेहैऔर अपनेघर चलेजातेहैऔर अपनेपेरेंट्स सेवोह लोग कुछ नही बतातेऔर फि र दबुारा सेवो लोग अगलेदि न मि लतेहैऔर उस बगं ्लो के अदं र जानेका डि साइड करतेहैऔर फि र वो लोग बगं लो अध्रं ेर जाय सेही जातेहैपहलेकी तरह आपनेआप गेट बन्द हो जाता हैफि र वो लोग डि साइड करतेहैइस बगं ्लो मैंअच्छेसेछन बि न करेगेफि र एक एक करके वो लोग अलग अलग होकर चान बि न करना शरु कर देतेहैफि र जब वो कि चन की तरफ पोचतेतब एक दम सेवो डर जातेहैक्यकुी पहलेजब वो कि चन मेंआय थेतब कुछ भी सम्मान नही था लेकीन जब वो अब कि चन में आय तो सम्मान था फि र उन्हेंसक हो जाता हैयह कोई न कोई तो जरूर रायता हैफि र वो और अच्छेसेछन बि न करना सरु कर

देतेहैंऔर नि ति न को कुछ पेपर मि लतेहैउसमेकोलकाता का एड्रसे लि खा होता हैसेम इस ही बगं लो की फ़ोटो इस पेपर मैंभी मि लती हैतो वो लोग सोचनेलगतेहैइस बगं लो की फोटो इस पेपर मैंक्या कर रही है!

2

फिर राहुल बोलता दोस्तो मझु लगता यही सेम बगं्लो कोलकाता मैतो नही चलो हमेकोलकाता चलकर देखना होगा और उसी लेटर मैंदो पासवर्ड भी लि खेथेफि र वो साम वालेफ्लाइट सेगांव सेकोलकाता के लि ए रवाना हो जातेहैजब वो लोग कोलकाता पहुंच जातेहैफिर वो उसी एड्रसे मैंपहुंच जातेहैजो एड्रसे उन्हेंपेपर पर मि ला था लेकि न जब वोह दरवाज़ा खोलतेहैतब वो खोल नही पातेक्यकुी वो पासवर्ड मांग रहा होता है फिर राहुल दो तीन बार पासवर्ड डलता हैलेकि न पासवर्ड गलत होता हैफि र अचानक सेनि ति न बोलता हैतमु वो वाला पासवर्ड डालकर देखो जो हमेउस पेपर पर मि ला था फिर राहुल बोलता हैअरे हां मैंतो भलू ी गया था फिर वोह पासवर्ड डालता लेकीन वो वाला भी पासवर्ड गलत होता हैफि र नि खि ल बोलता हैदसू रा वाला पासवर्ड डालकर ट्राई करो फि र जसैी ही वो दसू रा वाला पासवर्ड डालतेहैगेट घलु जाता हैफि र वो लोग अदं र जातेपहलेवालेघर की तरह इस बगं्लो का भी गेट अपनेआप बदं हो जाता हैऔर जि स तरह सेबगं्लो पहाड़ के पास बना हुआ था उसी तरह सेबगं्लो कोलकाता मैभी बना हुआ था और अधर सेभी सेम बना हुआ था फिर सेवो लोग उस बगं्लो मैंचान बि न करना शरुु कर देतेहैफि र राहुल खेता हैदोस्तो अगर हम उस आर्कि टेक के बारेमैपता चल जाए जि सनेयह गांव और कोलकाता का घर का माप बन आय हैतो हमेअगेका सबतू मि ल जाए गा फि र थोड़ी देर बाद उन्हेंएक नबंर मि ला हैऔर वो कि सी और का नही बल्की उसी आर्कटि क का होता हैफि र उसेवो लोग पछू तेहैकी जो कोलकाता का बगं्लो हैउसका माप आप नेही

बनया हैंवो कहता हैहा यह ऐसेदो घर है सेम जि सके माप मानेही बनया हैजो की बि लकुल सेम दि खतेहैफिर राहुल बोलता हैअच्छा अपको पता हैइस घर मैंकौन रेता था पहलेफि र वो बोलता हैजा तक मझु ेयाद हैइस घर मैंएक भड़ुिड़ियाहा रहती थी लेकि न मझु ेनहीं लगता अब वो जि दं ा होगी राहुल क्यों अपको क्यूनही लगता वो अभी जि दं ा होगी क्यकु े उसकी काफ़ी ज्यादा एज हो गयई थीं काफ़ी जायदा राहुल बोलता ठीक अकं ल इतनी इनफॉर्मेशि यो देनेके लि ए धन्यवाद फिर फोन कटनेके बाद वो लोग दबुारा चान बि न करना स्टार्ट कर देतेहैफि र नि ति न तजे सेअपनेदोस्तो को भलू ता हैऔर खेता हैयह देखो लाश फि र राहुल खेता हैअरेयेतो वहीं लाश हैजो हमेफोटो बेड के नीचेमि ली थी उनमेंसेएक बच्चा हैजायेशी लाश को उठातेहैंउसके कपड़ों के नि चेलि खा होता हैयह सेचलो जो ओ फि र वो सरेघर के बार नि कल आतेहैऔर आस पास पता करतेहै लेकीन कि सको नहींपता होता फि र एक बढ़ू ा आदमी नि कलता हैफि र नि खि ल उसेपछु ता हैअकं ल अपको पता हैहैं इस बगं् लो के बारेमेंकुछ फि र वो बढ़ू ा आदमी बोलता हैंहा मझु ेपता तो हैयह पर यह बगं् लो नही था तब एक महल था राजा का फि र नि खि ल बोलता हैंठीक हैअकं ल जी जानकारी देनेके लि ऐ सकु हरि या और फ़ि र राहुल अपने दोस्तो सेबोलता हैमझु ेपरुा यकीन हैयह पर कोई भतू नही हैमझु ेलगता हैकी यह पर कोई एक्टिं ग कर रहा है भतू की आवाज नि कालने की लेकि न मझु ेयह समझ नही आ राहा यह बच्चेकी लाश कहा सेआई चलो दोस्तो और भी चान बि न करतेहैफि र थोड़ी देर बाद नि खि ल को पेपर मि लता हैजब उसेखोलतेहैतो उसमेंकुछ लि खा नही होता कुछ भी बल्की एक माप मि लता हैफि र राहुल बोलता हैदोस्तो अब यह माप ही हमेभतू के पास तक ले जायेगा फि र वो लोग माप के सहरहेबगं लो के पीछेगार्डेनर्ड मेंपोहोच जातेहैऔर उन्हेंवहा पर कोनेमेंगफु ा दि खती हैफि र वो कूफा के अधर जातेऔर चलतेजातेचलतेजातेऔर गफु ा मेंउन्हेएक औरत की साड़ी मि लती हैऔर फि र और अगं ेजातेहैतो उन्हेंनकली बाल मि लतेहैऔरत के फ़ि र उनका सक यकीन मेंबदल जाता हैफि र और अगे जातेतो उन्हेकुछ आवाज सनु ई देती हैआदमीयो की बातेकरनेऔर राहुल बोलता हैदोस्तो रूक जोहो हम इनकी बातेसनु

तेहैफि र यह लोग बातेसनु तेहैतो वो आदमी बातेकर रहेथेकी क्या मस्त बेकुफ बनया हमनेउन लड़कों को अब वो कभी नही आयेगा और उन्हेंतो यह भी नही पता की हम यह लोग सोनेके जेवर के लिए कर रह

3

है आज हम उस जगह का पाता चल जायेगा जहा पर राजा का सारा जेवर मि ल जायेगा फिर यह सरेदोस्त जाके उन अदमि यो को पकड़ लेतेहैऔर उनसेकहतेऔर कोन कोन तमुहारेटीम मैंसामि ल हैफि र वो बोलते हैअच्छा हम बतातेहैऔर फिर वो बोलते है की हमारेएक और बधं ा है जो की भतू की एक्टिं ग कर रहा है और हम यह नाटक इसलि ए कर रहेथेकी हमेपता चल जाए की वो राजा का सोना कहा रखा हैफि र हम उसेपछू तेहैयह सोना खा पर है फि र वो बगं लो के पीछेएक बेसमेंट है वाहा पर यह सोना रखा है फि र हम लोग सोना जा रखा था वाहा पर जातेहैं और जब हम पोचतेथेतो वाहा पहलेजवानहेका भतू सत्र सोना रखा होता है और सोनेके पास एक बढ़िढिया गढ़ी होती है और वो हमेदेखकर भागनेलगती लेकीन हम भी उसके पीछेभागतेहैं और उसेपकड़ लेतेहैं फि र उसेपछू ते है पता इतना सारा सोना तरेपास कहा सेअय्या फि र वो वो बोल थी है पहलेयह पर एक राजा रेता था और उसके पास काफी ज्यादा सोना होता है फि र हम सोच लेतेहैं को इस राजा को हम मरदेगेऔर बगं ं लो मैंभतू की एक्टिं ग करेगेजि सकी वजह सेइस बगं ं लो मैंकोई नही आता था और आज हम यह सारा सोना लेकर भागनेवालेथेलेकि न तमु नेहमरा सारा प्लान चोपड़ा कर दि या फि र नि ति न बोलता हैअच्छा तमुहेउस छोटेसेबच्चेको क्यों मारा उसकी क्या गलती थी फि र बढ़िढिया बोलयेथी एक दि न हम सोनेको एक साइड कर रहेथेतब उस बच्चेनेदेख लि या था तो हमेलगा यह बच्चा कि सको बता ना देइसलि ए हमनेइस सेअपनेरास्तेसेही साफ कर दि या फि र हम लोग पलुलिस

को बलु ातहैऔर सारा सोना पलुलिस को देदेतेहैऔर इन लोगो को भी पलुलिस के आवलेकर देतेहै लेकि न जब यह लोग जेल झा रहेहोतेहैतो एक आदमी नि खि ल सेभलू ता हैतझु ेदेखलगूं ा दोस्तो abb सब कुछ ठीक हो जखु ा ता और जो लोगो को लग रहा था इस बगं लो मैंभतू वसैा कुछ नही इसलि ए सब कुछ ठीक होनेकी खशु ी मैंहम सरेदोस्त लोग डि साइड करतेहैकी कोई जगह पर गमु नेजाना चाहि ए और फीर सरेदोस्त बोलतेहै भाई बि लकुल सही बात हैफि र वोही सारेदोस्त बस स्टैंड के पास जा कर कड़ेहो जा थैहैलेकि न पहलेजब वोह घर सेनि कलेथेतब तो musam काफी जायदा और अच्छा था फि र जब वोह लोग बस स्टैंड के पास पछूं तेहैरात होने ही वालेहोती हैअचानक सेतजे बारि श होनेलगती हैऔर उन्हेबहुत देर बस का इंतजार करतेकरतेहो जाता है फि र वो लोग डि साइड करतेहैकी चलो मेट्रो से। चलतेहैऔर बारि श इतनी तजे हो रही थी की जब तक वो लोग मेट्रो स्टेशन पछूं तेहैतब उनके सारेगीलेहो जकेु थेक्यकूं बारि श बहुत ज्यादा तजे हो रही थी और रात भी हो जकुी थी और जब भी लोग मेट्रो स्टेशन के अदं र पछूं तेतो अजीब सी सतंं ति होती और कोई कोई भी दरू दरू तक मेट्रो स्टेशन मैंदि खई नही देराहा था फि र वोह सारेदोस्त जाकर मेट्रो जब प्लेटफार्म मैंआती हैतो सारेदोस्त जाकर मेट्रो मैंजाकर बठै जातेलेकि न मेट्रो काफी देर तक तो जल्दी रेती हैकही स्टेशन पर रुक थी हैलेकि न उस ट्रेन पर कोई नहीं बठै ा था और वोही फि र आगेजब ट्रेन जातेहैतब ही बार बार लाइट ट्रेन की ब्लि गं करनेलग जाति हैतो सारेदोस्त काफी जायद डर जातेहैडर के मारेछि लनेलगातेलेकि न फि र उन्हेंएक परचाया दि खाए देथी हैऔर वाहा सेसदुंर सेलड़की चली आ रही थी फि र राहुल हि च की चाचेहुए उसका नाम पछू ता तो वाहा बोलती हैमेरा नाम पायल हैऔर वो इतनेजायदा हॉट होतेहैकी नि ति न तो उसको देखतेही रहेजाता हैफि र पायल नि ति न को हि लतेहुए बोल थी हैओह हेलो तमुहेक्या हो गया नि ति न बोलता हैफि र नही नहीं मझुे कुछ नही हुआ और फीर woho nitin ke pass Jaa कर बठै जाती मेट्रो टेंपरेचर जायदा इसके वजह सेउसेठंड भी लगनेलगती हैइसलि ए नि ति न अपनी जकैं ट उतार कर उस लडकी को देदेता हैलेकि न दोस्तो जो कुछ नि ति न के साथ हुआ हैवो कोई

लड़की नहीं बल्कि नि ति न एक सपनेमैंको सखु ा था और नि ति न के सारेदोस्त नि ति न सेपछू तेओय तझु ेक्या हो गया था तो नि ति न चि लतेहुए बोलता हैवोही लड़की कहा गया वोही लड़की कहा गया फि र सरे दोस्त kunse

4

लड़की यह पर तो कोई नही हैजररूर तन्नू कोई सपना देखा होगा फि
र एज स्टेशन मैंजा कर मेट्रो रुकतेहैतो नि ति न को वोही लड़की
सीडी सेअप्पर जातेहुए दि खाए देथी हैऔर वोही सि र्फ नि ति न को
नहींबल्कि उसके सारे दोस्तो को भी दी खाए देती हैऔर उसके सारेदोस्त
डरतेडरतेबोलतेहैइस मेट्रो स्टेशन मैंतो कोई ak सि क्रूटी guard bhi
nahi दि खा रहा फि र यह लड़की मेट्रो स्टेशन मैंअकेलेक्या कर रही हैफि
र जब सारेदोस्त भागतेहुए उस लड़की के पास पछू तेतो वो लड़की गायब
हो जकु ी होती हैयह सब देखकर सारेदोस्त बहुत डर जातेहैंऔर मेट्रो के
बाहर बाद मैंलग जातेहैंऔर वहांपर उन्हेंएक ऑटो खड़ा दि खता हैऔर
उस ऑटो सेलड़की हाथ नि काले होती हैऔर हेल्प हेल्प चि ल्ला रही होती
हैयह सब सनु कर नि ति न का मन उसेबचानेका करता हैलेकि न जब
तक नि ति न और नि ति न के दोस्त ऑटो के पास पहुंचतेहैंऑटो तजे
रफ्तार मैंआगेचला गया होता हैऔर फि र थोड़ी देर बाद नि ति न और
नि ति न के दोस्त को एक और ऑटो दि खता हैऔर वह आदमी आराम
सेऑटो मेंबठै ा सो रहा होता हैऔर फि र सारे दोस्त उसेचि ल्लातेहुए
बोलतेहैंकि भयै ा जल्दी करो इस ऑटो का पीछा करो और आप जि
तनेभी पसैं मांगोगेहम आप लोग को देंगेऔर फि र ऑटो का पीछा करत-
करतेआगेपहुंच जातेहैंलेकि न ऑटो सेकाफी ज्यादा दरू था लेकि न नि
ति न और नि ति न के दोस्त कभी ऑटो के पास आ जाए और कभी ऑटो
सेदरू चला जाए और फि र वह लोग एक पलु के पास पहुंच जातेहैंऔर
ऑटो सेउस लड़की को उठाकर फेंक देतेहैंपानी में और यह सब ऑटोवाला

देखकर तुरंत पुलिस को फोन लगा देता हैऔर जब पुलिस आती हैतो कि सी तरह नि ति न को तो बचा लेती हैक्योंकि वह भी उस लड़की को बचानेके लि ए पानी मेंखनू गया था और पुलिस वालेलड़की को नहीं बचा पातेऔर पुलिस वालेनि ति न को हॉस्पि टल लेजातेहैंऔर अगली सबु ह जब होती हैतो नि ति न अपने दोस्तों सेऔर पुलिस वालेसेपछू ता हैलड़की ठीक तो हैना लेकि न जो पुलिस वाला होता हैवह नि ति न के दोस्तों और उसका नि ति न का दोस्त होता हैतो बोलता हैअरेयार वहां लड़की लड़की कम सेकम एक महीना पहलेमर चकु ी हैउसी पानी मेंजाकर और तमु उसी के पीछेभागतेरहतेहो और हम तमुहें1 महीनेसेसमझानेकी कोशि श कर रहे हैंकि वह लड़की बहुत पहलेमर चकु ी हैलेकि न तमु समझनेको तयै ार ही नहीं हो और यह सब सनु रहा होता हैगेट के बाहर खड़ेहुए ऑटो वाला ऑटो वाला कार्ड सेबोलता हैकि आज मैंफर्स्ट नहींजाऊंगा क्योंकि यही लड़के बोल रहेथेकि उस ऑटो का पीछा करो तो वह आठ वाला बोलता हैअरेतमुहेंकुछ नहीं होगा वह साहब का दोस्त हैऔर पहलेवह लड़की सेप्यार करता था और वह अब मर गई हैऔर उसी के पीछेयह भागता रहता हैतमु चि तं ा मत करो तमुहेंकुछ नहीं होगा दोस्तों अगर आपको कुछ थोड़ी अच्छी लगी हो तो जरूर सेसपोर्ट करना

Ansh Sharma